For the loves that survive the power outages — literal and metaphorical.

Table of Contents

The Night Everything Went Dark

..∞ · ✲ ◗ ▷

She was halfway to freedom when the lights went out on Saturday night.

Marissa had planned everything—lawyer on Monday, apartment by Thursday, life rebooted by Christmas. But the storm moved faster than she did. Snow clawed at the kitchen windows. Her reflection wavered in the glass—deep brown skin, a beauty mark by her left brow, her grandmother's cheekbones now drawn with fatigue. The divorce papers waited in her laptop bag.

Twenty years together, and this was how it ended: in the dark, with him still in the next room.

"Power's out?" Gregory's voice came from the living room, where he'd been watching the Knicks game.

"You think?" She bit back the rest of her response. No point starting another fight. Not when she was leaving in a few days.

She heard him moving through the darkness, his footsteps sure even without light. Gregory never stumbled, never hesitated. Everything calculated, controlled. Even now, she could picture his jaw tight with irritation at the inconvenience.

"I'll check the circuit breaker," he said.

"It's the storm. The whole street's dark."

"I'll check anyway."

Always had to verify everything himself. Never trusted her judgment. Her two-strand twisted curls brushed her cheeks as she hunted for matches — she'd left them somewhere, same as she left cabinet doors open, drawers half-done, thoughts half-finished.

"Ah ha!" She found them above the stove and lit the vanilla candles she kept for her evening baths. Soft light pooled on the granite countertops they'd argued about for weeks. He wanted black. She wanted white. They compromised on gray with black and white speckles.

The basement door slammed. She checked her phone. Two percent battery. *Perfect.* She'd meant to charge it, but got distracted making calls about the women's shelter's heating bill. There was always something that needed fixing for somebody else.

Gregory's phone sat on the coffee table. Dead too. He'd probably drained it scrolling through emails during dinner, answering work questions between bites of her jerk chicken. The same chicken recipe her grandmother taught her, the one he used to beg for when they were broke newlyweds in that roach-infested apartment in New Haven. Then, he sucked the sauce off his fingers and praised her cooking. Now, only the obligatory "Thanks for dinner" signaled that he was aware she had prepared it.

"Breaker's fine," he announced, brushing snow from his shoulders. "We should have bought that generator."

"We should have done a lot of things."

He paused in the doorway, his face half-shadowed in the candlelight. At forty-five, Gregory was no longer the earnest pre-med student she'd met at her cousin's barbecue. When he smiled, the small gap between his front teeth showed, rare as it was lately. Broader now, gray threading through his close-cut beard, but with those same dark eyes that used to see right through her. *When did they stop looking?*

"You okay?" he asked.

"Fine."

"You don't sound fine."

"Since when do you notice how I sound?"

He exhaled through his nose, that controlled breath he did instead of arguing. "I'm trying here, Marissa."

"Now you're trying? Tonight? When the power's out and you can't escape to your precious gym or office or wherever else you disappear to?"

"That's not how I see it."

"Really?" She laughed, sharp and bitter. "When's the last time you were home for dinner three nights in a row? When's the last time we talked about something other than bills or your mother or which charity gala you're refusing to attend this time?"

"I work. I provide. That's what I do."

"Nobody asked you to kill yourself providing."

"You think the mortgage pays itself? Think your community center runs on good intentions?"

"My community center? It's for families who need help, Gregory. Remember needing help? Or did you forget where we came from?"

"I didn't forget anything. That's why I work so hard. So we never go back there."

"We were happy there."

"We were broke."

"We worked together, even when you abandoned the medical field and switched to business management."

Silence stretched between them. Outside, wind rattled the windows they'd replaced last spring. Top of the line, energy efficient, like everything else in this house. All the best things money could buy, except time with each other.

"I'm getting more candles," Marissa said.

She moved past him toward the hallway closet, but his hand caught her wrist. Not hard, but enough to stop her. *When was the last time he'd touched her on purpose?*

"Wait," he said. "Wait."

THE NIGHT EVERYTHING WENT DARK

What We Don't Say

..⊕ · ✳ ● ▷

Gregory released her wrist but didn't step back. In the flickering light, Marissa could see the calculation in his eyes, the same look he got when reviewing portfolios or planning his workout routine. *Constantly analyzing, never feeling.*

"We need to talk," he said.

"Now you want to talk? The one night you literally can't go anywhere else?"

"That's the second time you've said that. Where exactly do you think I go?"

Marissa turned away, but the darkness made escape impossible. Every direction led back to this moment, this room, this man she'd promised to love forever. "Does it matter?"

"If you're accusing me of something, yes, it matters."

"I'm not accusing. I'm..." She pressed her palms against her eyes. "I'm tired, Gregory. Bone tired. And not from staying up waiting anymore."

"What's that supposed to mean?"

"Nothing. Get the candles yourself."

She felt her way to the kitchen, muscle memory guiding her to the stove. The pot of soup she'd made earlier had gone cold. No way to reheat it now. She lifted the lid and sniffed. Split pea with ham hocks, his favorite. *Why did she still cook his favorites?*

Gregory followed her, bringing one of the candles. He set it on the counter between them like a peace offering. "Remember when we lost power in New Haven? That ice storm junior year?"

"We played cards until four in the morning."

"You cheated at spades."

"I did not cheat. You just can't count."

His smile flickered briefly. "You wore my Howard sweatshirt and those fuzzy socks with the holes in them."

"It was freezing. The radiator barely worked on good days."

"We made it work though."

"We were kids. We didn't know better."

"Maybe knowing better is overrated."

Marissa studied his face in the candlelight. This version of Gregory, soft around the edges, almost looked like the boy who used to walk her to class, carrying her books even though his load was heavier. *When did he become this stranger in an expensive suit?*

"Do you remember what you said when you proposed?" she asked.

His shoulders tensed. "Marissa..."

"You said we'd have a house full of kids. Said you'd never be like Robert, never be the man who came home just to sleep. You promised."

"We tried. The doctors said…"

"We could have adopted. Could still adopt. But you always had a reason to wait. The promotion, the house, the market. Those things were not more important. They were excuses."

"That's not true."

"Then why are we still just two people in this big empty house?"

Gregory moved around the counter, closing the space she'd carefully maintained. "You think I don't want that? Think I don't lie awake wondering what our kids would look like? Whether they'd have your smile or my stubborn streak?"

"You lie awake? When? Between your 5 AM gym session and your midnight emails?"

"You're being unfair."

"Stop saying that word like it means something. Fair. Nothing about this is fair. Not the way you shut me out, not the way I pretend not to notice the perfume on your shirts…"

"What? What perfume? Marissa, what are you talking about?"

She turned to face him fully. "Tuesday. You came home smelling like gardenias. You hate gardenias. Said they remind you of funeral homes."

"I was looking at houses with Carol from the firm. We were investigating properties for a portfolio of REITs. She practically bathes in that flowery stuff. You know this. You've met Carol. She's sixty years old and married to a rabbi."

"Yes, Carol. At the summer picnic she made it a point of sharing with me how buff you are. She's sixty, but works out at the same time you do. That woman, married or not, seems to have mapped every muscle on your body. It was a super weird and uncomfortable conversation."

"She is only a colleague to me, Marissa. I have no idea what her body looks like. At the gym, I'm focused on me."

"At the gym? Well, last Thursday, you said you were at the gym but your gym bag was still in your car..."

"I keep spare clothes in my office. I've told you that a hundred times. After I split my pants during the Henderson presentation..."

"And there it is. The reasonable explanation. You pull them out so conveniently, and it never changes a thing."

"Because they're true! Marissa, I'm not cheating on you. I'm barely home enough to sleep, so when would I have time for an affair?"

"That's exactly my point."

The words hung between them, heavy as the snow piling against their windows. Gregory's face went through several expressions before settling on something she hadn't seen in years. Hurt. Raw and uncomplicated.

A Thousand Ordinary Days

..∞ · ❄ ◗ ▷

"You'd rather I was cheating," Gregory said quietly. "That would be easier, wouldn't it? Clear cut. A reason to leave that everyone would understand."

Marissa's chest tightened. "Don't."

"But this? This is messier. What we have is twenty years of small failures. Death by a thousand ordinary days."

"Stop."

"No, let's get real, Marissa. I bury myself in work because it's easier than coming home to a house that doesn't know laughter anymore. And you? You sign up for every charity event in Connecticut because if you stop moving, you might have to feel how empty it all is."

"Gregory, please."

"This is us turning into everything we swore we wouldn't become. And the worst part? We did it together. We chose avoidance every single day. Didn't we?"

The candle between them flickered, throwing wild shadows on the walls. Marissa gripped the counter's edge until her knuckles ached. He was right. God help her, he was right. An affair would have been simpler. Instead, this was all that remained: a marriage reduced to proximity, not presence, and two people orbiting the ghost of what they once were.

"I made an appointment," she said. "With a lawyer. For Monday."

Gregory nodded slowly, like he'd been expecting it. Maybe he had. "Okay."

"Okay? That's it?"

"What do you want me to say? That I'm surprised? That I didn't see you pulling away every time I reached for you? That I don't notice how you tense up when I walk in the door?"

"I don't…"

"You do. Even your shoulders change. Like you're bracing for disappointment."

She wanted to deny it, but the words wouldn't come. When had she started steeling herself against him? When had home become a place to endure rather than enjoy?

"I hate how you chew," she blurted out.

Gregory blinked. "What?"

"Your chewing. It drives me crazy. You chew like you're punishing the food. Like eating is just another task to power through."

"My chewing? Twenty years and you're leaving over how I chew?"

"No, I'm leaving because we're strangers who happen to share a mortgage. The chewing is… it's all of it. It's every little thing that used to be endearing and now reminds me how far apart we've drifted."

Gregory was quiet for a long moment. Then: "You snore. These little whistling sounds. Like a broken teakettle."

"I do not snore."

"You do. And you leave cabinet doors open. Every single one. I follow behind you, closing them like some kind of kitchen ghost."

"You alphabetize the spice rack."

"You put wet towels on the bed."

"You time your showers."

"You reorganize my desk."

"You throw away my magazines before I've read them."

"You keep magazines for six months without reading them!"

They stared at each other across the candlelit counter, breathing hard like they'd been fighting with fists instead of facts. Those open doors, the half-folded laundry, the trail of mugs—all proof of her mind leaping ahead of her hands. He knew this about her. Then Gregory's mouth twitched. A sound escaped him, half laugh, half sob.

"Listen to us," he said. "Twenty years of grievances, all saved up like frequent flyer miles."

Despite everything, Marissa felt her own mouth curve slightly. "When did we stop saying these things with love?"

"When we stopped saying them at all."

The house groaned under the weight of snow. Somewhere in the walls, wood settled and adjusted. Marissa thought about their first apartment, how every sound had been an adventure, every quirk a discovery. Now she knew this house's every sigh and could predict Gregory's every move. Mystery had been replaced by routine, worn smooth as river stones.

"I'm cold," she said.

"Fire's going in the living room. Should last a few more hours if we're careful."

They moved together toward the warmth, bringing candles to light their way. The living room felt smaller in the dancing shadows, more like the cramped spaces they'd shared when every stick of furniture had a story and every dollar had a purpose.

Truth or Dare

..⊙ · ✳ ◗ ▷

Gregory added the last decent log to the fire while Marissa settled onto the couch, pulling the throw blanket around her shoulders. The same blanket his mother had crocheted for their fifth anniversary. Back when Delores still liked her, before the comments about grandchildren became barbs instead of hints.

"She asks about you," Gregory said, reading her mind the way he used to. "Mom. Every Sunday when I call."

"What do you tell her?"

"That you're busy. Saving the world one fundraiser at a time."

"While you're saving it one fund under management at a time?"

"Last time we saw her, she waited until you went to the kitchen to say, 'All that caring and still no one calling you daddy.' I should've said something, but I didn't."

Marissa blinked hard, willing the tears to retreat before they gave her away. "You didn't have to. She said it for both of you."

"Something like that." He sat in his chair across from her, the leather one she'd surprised him with after his first big promotion. They'd celebrated on it that night, christening it in ways that would scandalize the furniture store. Now he looked tired in it, older,

16

shoulders curved inward like parentheses around an unfinished thought.

"Remember what we used to do during storms?" Marissa asked suddenly, trying to change the subject.

"Truth or dare."

"You always picked dare."

"You always made me do embarrassing things."

"That was the point."

They sat quietly, watching the fire consume the last log. Without discussing it, they both knew this was it. No more wood. No more heat after this. Just darkness and cold and whatever came next. He absently tapped the glucose monitor on his arm, the small beeping reminder that discipline had kept him alive this long.

"Truth or dare?" Gregory whispered.

Marissa pulled the blanket tighter. "We're too old for games."

"We're too old for a lot of things. Doesn't mean we stop."

She considered him across the narrowing space, this man who'd shared her bed for two decades but hadn't shared her thoughts in years. "Truth."

"When did you stop loving me?"

"That's not... I never stopped loving you."

"Truth, Marissa. You picked truth."

She closed her eyes, feeling for words that wouldn't cut too deep. "I don't know if I stopped loving you or

17

if I just stopped remembering what loving you felt like. It's like… like trying to recall the taste of something you haven't eaten in years. You know you enjoyed it once, but the memory's just…. just fading."

"So your love for me has faded?"

"Hasn't yours faded for me? We seem to be shadows of the people we once were, the couple we were supposed to become."

Gregory leaned forward, elbows on his knees. "Your turn."

"Truth or dare?"

"Truth."

"Why the gym? Really. Not the surface answer about health or looking good. Why do you spend two hours there every morning instead of two minutes here with me?"

He was quiet for so long she thought he might refuse to answer. The fire popped, sending sparks up the chimney. When he spoke, his voice was rougher than she'd heard in years.

"Control. At the gym, I control everything. The weight, the reps, the progress. If I'm weak, I get stronger. If I fail, I try again tomorrow. Clear metrics. Definable success." He looked up at her. "Nothing like marriage. Nothing like trying to figure out why my wife flinches when I reach for her or how to fill a silence that used to be comfortable. The gym doesn't require emotional intelligence I never learned because I was too busy making sure we'd never be poor again."

"We were never poor. We were just broke. There's a difference."

"Not to a kid who watched his mother water down milk to make it last. Not to a man who promised himself his family would never know that feeling."

"But I'm not the family you grew up in, Gregory. That's the problem. It's just me, and I knew that feeling of wanting. I lived it with you in the early days of our marriage. It didn't scare me the way it scared you."

"Everything scares me when it comes to you."

The truth settled between them, too heavy to take back. Marissa shifted, letting the blanket fall open. "Since when?"

"Since the first time you smiled at me. Since you took my hand at Keisha's barbecue like it was nothing, like touching me was the most natural thing in the world. Since you made me believe I could be more than Robert's stepson who better not fuck up."

"You were always more than that."

"Not to me. Not until you."

Something True

..⊕ · ❋ ❥ ▷

The fire was dying. They could both see it, the way the flames shrank back like a red-hot tide going out. Soon there would be nothing but embers, then ash, then cold.

"We could burn the chairs," Marissa suggested, half-joking.

"Start with mine. You always hated that chair."

"I bought you that chair."

"Doesn't mean you didn't hate it." Gregory stood, pacing to the window. The snow had covered everything, erasing the familiar landmarks of their neighborhood. "Can't see the Petersons' house. Or the street."

"We're stuck."

Stuck. She said the word before realizing all the meanings layered in it. *Stuck in this house, in this storm, in this marriage...*

"I used to love snow days," she said. "The unexpected freedom. Permission to stop everything and just be."

"When's the last time we just were?"

"I don't know. Maybe that trip to Oak Bluffs? Your fortieth?"

"You spent half that trip on the phone with the community center. The boiler issue."

"You spent the other half checking market reports."

"We're really bad at vacations."

"We're bad at a lot of things."

Gregory turned from the window. In the dying firelight, shadows carved deep lines around his mouth, his eyes. *When had he started looking so worn? When had she stopped noticing?*

"Gregory?"

"Yes, Marissa?"

"Tell me something else that's true. Something you've never said out loud."

He moved back toward the couch and sat near her, but stopped just outside the blanket's reach.

"I practice conversations with you. In the car on my way to work. At the gym in my head as I lift. Lying in bed while you sleep. All the things I want to say, but can't figure out how to start. I've had entire arguments, apologies, declarations. Won some, lost others. But when I actually see you, the words... evaporate."

"I'm going to ignore the creepiness of you watching me while I sleep for a minute. What kind of conversations?"

"All kinds. Small stuff mostly. Like how I saw a cardinal at lunch and remembered you saying they were your grandmother's favorite. Or how the new guy at work reminds me of your cousin Marcus, the one who tried to fight me at our wedding."

"He was drunk. And protective."

"He was right, though. Said I'd hurt you eventually. Just took longer than he thought."

"Gregory..."

"I practice telling you about my day. A real, animated reenactment of some of the stupid stuff, not the sterilized one-liner. How I hate most of my clients, how the money stopped mattering years ago, but I don't know how to stop chasing it. Marissa..."

She waited.

"I'm afraid if I slow down, I'll realize I spent all this time building the wrong life."

She inhaled sharply, her body leaning toward him before she even realized she'd moved.

"Why don't you tell me these things?"

"Because you're already disappointed in who I became. Why add to the list?"

Marissa stood, the blanket falling to the couch. "You think I'm disappointed in you?"

"Aren't you? I became exactly what we used to mock. Corporate drone in a suit worth more than our first car, scheduling life around conference calls and quarterly reports. Remember how we laughed at those guys?"

"We were kids."

"We were right."

She moved close enough to see the fine lines around his eyes, the scar on his chin from a bike accident their second year together. "I suppose I am disappointed... with us. Both of us. We had all these plans, all these dreams, and we traded them for financial security and separate lives that happen to intersect at this address."

"The adoption papers are still in my desk," he said quietly. "Top drawer. I look at them sometimes, wondering what would happen if I just filled them out. If I came home with them completed and said, 'Let's do this, let's be the family we always talked about.'"

"Why don't you?"

"Same reason you don't ask about them. We can't even manage us, Marissa. How could we manage a child who needs more than we're giving each other?"

SOMETHING TRUE

Body Heat

..∞ · ❄ ❥ ▷

The truth just sank in, quiet and deep. He'd checked the insulin packs before the power died. This habit of his was now a quiet vigilance she rarely noticed anymore. Marissa reached for his hand, surprised when he let her take it. His palm was rough, calloused from the weights he lifted religiously.

"Your hands are freezing," he said.

"Everything's freezing."

"Come here."

He pulled her against him, awkward at first, like teenagers learning to dance. She couldn't remember the last time they'd spooned like this, her head fitting perfectly under his chin, his arms creating a space just for her. Her hands, always expressive even mid-argument, now rested against his chest, finally still. He still smelled the same underneath the expensive cologne. Like soap and something uniquely Gregory, something that used to make her feel safe.

"This is weird," she mumbled against his chest.

"Yeah."

"When did hugging my husband become weird?"

"Probably around the same time we started scheduling sex."

"We don't schedule sex."

"We don't have sex to schedule."

She pulled back enough to see his face. "Whose fault is that?"

"Does it matter? We're here now. Frozen in our expensive house with our separate lives and our polite distance. Keeping score won't warm us up."

The last of the fire collapsed into itself, sending up a final shower of sparks. Darkness crept closer, held back only by the few candles still burning. Their phones were dead, the power was out, and the snow had trapped them in this museum of their marriage.

"I'm scared," Marissa said.

"Of the dark?"

"Of the morning. Of what Monday means. Of signing papers that turn twenty years into a division of assets. Of being forty-three and starting over. Of finding out this is the best I could do."

Gregory's arms tightened around her. "You could do better. You know that, right? Find someone who comes home for dinner, who chooses you over the gym, who doesn't need to practice conversations in his head."

"Someone who doesn't hate charity galas?"

"Someone who loves them. Who bids on every silent auction item and doesn't complain about the rubber chicken dinners."

"Someone who wants kids as much as I do?"

"A whole houseful of older kids in need of love. Soccer practice and piano lessons and science fairs."

"Someone who doesn't chew too loud?"

Despite everything, she felt him smile against her hair. "Someone perfect."

"I don't want perfect." The words surprised her as much as him. "I had perfect on paper. Young love, shared dreams, promises under stars. Look where perfect got us."

"Then what do you want?"

She thought about the divorce papers in her bag, the apartment she'd already scouted near the community center, the life she'd planned that looked exactly like this one minus him. "I want to stop being so tired. I want to stop pretending we're okay when we're drowning in silence. I want..."

"What?"

"I want my friend back. Before the husband, before the provider, before whatever we've become. I want the guy who made me laugh until my stomach hurt, who talked to me about everything and nothing until the sun came up. I want conversations that don't feel like negotiations."

"That guy might be gone, Marissa."

"Is he though? Because five minutes ago you made a joke about burning furniture. And right now you're holding me like it matters, not like it's an obligation. Maybe he's not gone. Maybe he's buried under all the things we thought were important. Perhaps... he's changed."

"And if we dig him out? Then what? We pretend the last decade didn't happen?"

"No. We admit it did. We admit we fucked up, got lost, turned into people we don't particularly like. And then we decide if that's where the story ends."

Remembering How

..∞ · ❋ ❨ ▷

Gregory was quiet for so long she could hear his heartbeat, steady and familiar. The fire had been dead for nearly half an hour now, and the cold was starting to claim the room—edges first, then deeper, a slow invasion through the walls.

They stayed like that anyway, arms uncertain at first, learning how to hold each other again. The silence wasn't empty this time—it was recalibration. Breath syncing. Warmth rediscovered. When the chill crept closer, they tightened their embrace, sharing what little heat they had left.

When he finally spoke, his voice came from somewhere deeper than usual, a place she remembered from late-night talks in their first apartment.

"I see him sometimes. The guy I used to be. In mirrors at the gym, or store windows when I'm rushing to a meeting. Just glimpses. He looks... confused, like he took a wrong turn and can't figure out how to get back."

"Gregory?"

"Yeah?"

She smiled faintly. "Why are you talking about yourself like that?"

He huffed out a laugh. "Because it's easier than saying it's me. Feels safer, I guess."

They both chuckled, the sound small but real.

"I could get used to that," he said.

"What?"

"Us. Laughing again. Existing in the same space without fighting the air."

She let the quiet stretch a little before asking, "So what would that guy — the one you see — say if he could talk to you?"

Gregory ran a hand over his jaw. "He'd probably ask why I own seven suits but only one good memory from the past year. Why I can recite my A1C and cholesterol numbers but not your favorite song. Why I... why I worked so hard to protect us from being broke but not from being strangers."

Marissa's eyes softened. "My favorite song is still the same."

"'Golden,'" he said without hesitation. "Jill Scott."

She nodded. "You remember."

"I remember everything from before. It's the after that gets fuzzy. Like there's this line somewhere around year ten where we stopped creating memories and started maintaining schedules."

Marissa pulled back, needing to see him. The candlelight was almost gone, but she could still make out his face — bare, unguarded, the man beneath the armor he wore to board meetings and family dinners.

"Then what are we doing now, Gregory?" she asked quietly.

He hesitated. "Trying, I think. Or maybe just... remembering how."

"Remembering how to what?"

"How to be us." He ran a hand through his hair, exhaling hard. "I don't have some speech ready, Marissa. I've practiced a hundred conversations in my head, but none of them sound right when I'm actually here with you."

She waited, saying nothing.

"I want…" He stopped, rubbed the back of his neck. "God, I don't even know the right words. I want you to stay, but not because of habit or guilt or the storm. I want you to stay because maybe we're not finished yet."

"That's not fair."

"You hate that word," he said, a sad smile flashing. "But tell me — when was love ever fair? It'd be easier if I fell for someone who didn't leave cabinets open or run charity events during playoff season. Easier to love someone who fit neatly into my life instead of blowing holes in it. But that's not what I want. I want you and me… this union to be real."

"Were," she said softly. "We *were* real."

"Only if we let it stay past tense."

She shook her head. "You can't fix a crack, years in the making, in one night because the power went out, and we ran out of places to hide."

"I know." He met her eyes. "But I can start. Tomorrow, I skip the gym. I make breakfast — not green smoothies. Monday, you cancel the lawyer and make an appointment with a counselor. We stop pretending the distance is permanent."

"And then what? We forget tonight?"

"No," he said, voice rough. "We remember. We remember almost losing everything and choosing not to. We remember that under all the noise, I still know your favorite song and you still know mine. We remember that I still want to hold you when you're cold, and you still miss your friend. That's not nothing."

"I don't know if I can do it again," she whispered. "Try, fail, and end up right back here."

He nodded slowly. "Then we end up here. But at least we'll tell the kids we didn't quit easy."

She blinked at him. "What kids?"

"The ones we were supposed to have," he said quietly. "The ones we'll adopt. The ones who'll roll their eyes at us when we pull them into a group hug. The ones who'll need to see that love isn't flawless, just willing."

Tears rose in her eyes, hot and uninvited. "You can't just say things like that."

"Why not? What's left to lose? You were halfway gone already." He swallowed, frustrated. "Look, I don't have the language for this. I just know I want my life with you."

"Gregory…"

"I know," he said before she could finish. "I've been awful. Not just lately, probably for years. I chose work over us, the gym over conversation, control over closeness. But when the lights went out tonight, the only person I wanted to be trapped with was you."

34

He stopped, his voice catching. "That has to mean something…. It means something, Marissa!"

Love Plus

..∞ · ❀ ❯ ▷

The tears came then, spilling over cheeks in the dark. Marissa didn't try to stop them, just let them fall while Gregory held her, his own breathing suspiciously unsteady.

"I signed up for pottery classes," she said against his chest.

"What?"

"Three months ago. Tuesday nights. You never asked where I went."

"I assumed community center stuff."

"No. Pottery. I'm terrible at it. Everything comes out lopsided and ugly. But for two hours a week, I get to create something with my hands. Something that doesn't require committee approval or donor management or pretending everything's fine when it's not. The wheel calms me. The rhythm, the mess, the way it asks for presence. It's the only place my brain stops sprinting."

"Can I see them? The things you made?"

"They're in the basement. Hidden behind the Christmas decorations you never help me put up."

"I'll help this year."

"Don't make promises you can't keep."

"You're right. Um. I can put together a world-music holiday playlist and keep the spiked cider flowing. I'll try my best."

She smiled at that, then pulled back to see him. In the one-stump-of-a-candle-lit room, they could still make out the outlines of each other, the curve of a shoulder, the shape of breath. "And what if trying isn't enough?" she asked softly. "What if we're already too far apart, too set in our separate ways?"

"Then at least our divorce will have better stories. 'Remember the time we tried pottery together and we both somehow got clay everywhere?' Instead of 'We just drifted apart.'"

"You want to take pottery with me?"

"I want to do life with you. Pottery, charity galas, burning furniture when the power goes out. All of it. The question is whether you want that too."

"Love isn't always enough."

"Marissa. No, but it's a start. Love plus pottery. Love plus breakfast. Love plus actually talking instead of managing logistics. Love plus remembering we chose each other for reasons that had nothing to do with financial security or perfect houses."

"Love plus dealing with your mother asking about grandchildren?"

"Love plus finally telling her we're working on it. That we've got applications ready, just needed to find our way back to each other first."

"Love plus you coming home for dinner?"

"Love plus me cooking dinner sometimes. Badly, but trying."

"Love plus therapy?"

"Love plus …whatever it takes."

The last candle flickered out, leaving them in complete darkness. Outside, the storm continued its work, erasing the world they knew, covering every familiar landmark with something new. Marissa could hear nothing but their breathing and the settling bones of their house.

"I can't see you," she said.

"I'm here."

"Promise?"

"Truth or dare?"

"Truth."

"Marissa, I'm here. I've been here. Even when I was at the gym or the office or lost in my own head. Part of me has always been here, waiting for you to call me back."

"Then why didn't you say something?"

"Same reason you didn't. Fear. Pride. The weight of accumulated silence. It's easier to maintain distance than risk reaching out and finding nothing there."

"But you're reaching now."

"Can we both reach for each other? Question is whether we're brave enough to hold on."

In the absolute darkness, without the distractions of screens or schedules, Marissa felt herself soften, the fight in her giving way to something gentler. Not healing exactly, but the possibility of it. The recognition that the man holding her wasn't a stranger after all, just someone who'd gotten as lost as she had in the business of building a life that looked good from the outside.

"I'm cold," she said.

"Body heat's all we've got left."

"Then we'd better get closer."

They fumbled their way to the bedroom, muscle memory and whispered directions guiding them. The comforter wasn't much against the dropping temperature, but wrapped around both of them it held their shared warmth. Marissa tucked her feet under his legs, the way she used to in the early days of their marriage.

"Your feet are ice," he complained without moving away.

"It's your fault for not buying a generator."

"Our fault. We make decisions together, remember? Or we used to."

"We could start again. Making decisions together."

"Starting tomorrow?"

"Starting now."

He reached down and grabbed her hands, his grip sure. "Marissa," he said softly, "if there's still anything left in us, anything at all, then let's do this. Not because we remember who we were, but because we might still be more than what we became. I don't want perfect. I just want honesty. I want the version of us that stays when it would be easier to walk away."

She looked at him for a long moment, the darkness hiding nothing now. "Then let's start small," she whispered. "One morning at a time. One conversation at a time. We'll see if what's left can grow."

He nodded. She brushed her thumb across the line of his jaw, feeling the rough stubble. He caught her hand and turned it, pressing a slow kiss into her palm. The gesture was so simple, so familiar, that something unlatched inside her.

When he leaned closer, their noses bumped. He laughed — quiet, uncertain. "I forgot how to do this," he admitted.

"Then don't think about it," she said. "You're always thinking."

"And you never do," he teased, his voice easing back into that playful register she'd missed.

"Exactly." She guided his hand to her face. "Let it be unplanned for once."

Their lips met tentatively, a testing of ground long left fallow. The kiss deepened not from hunger but from recognition, the slow remembering of rhythm and breath. His hand slid to her shoulder, her fingers found the back of his neck, and the space between them dissolved.

Later, when the room had gone utterly still except for the wind outside, they lay side by side, breath mingling, laughter soft as the snow settling beyond the window.

"I used to like that you never made plans," he said.

"You used to like proving you could."

"Maybe we needed both."

"Maybe we still do."

He reached for her again, this time without hesitation, and she let him, surprised at how natural it felt—not a grand rekindling, but the quiet return of something that had never fully died.

When the Lights Came On

..oœ · ✳ ◗ ▷

The lights snapped on.

After hours of darkness, the glare was violent—every corner exposed, every shadow erased.

Marissa jerked upright. Gregory squinted beside her, blinking against the brightness. For one suspended breath, they remained motionless next to each other, dazed by the sudden return of electricity and everything it implied.

Then, both moved at once.

She went for her phone; he went for his. Screens flared to life, charging lights pulsing like tiny heartbeats on their nightstands. The ordinary fuss of power restored, but this time it felt like an intrusion.

A ringtone cut through the room.

Gregory's.

He glanced at the screen and froze. "It's Carol."

Marissa's pulse stumbled. *Of course, it was Carol*—the bold white female, invading her marriage, smelling of gardenias and blurred professional lines.

The phone kept ringing. Gregory silenced it and set it back in its charging cradle.

"It's Sunday morning," Marissa said evenly.

"Probably work."

"She always works through weekends, during a blizzard? She expects you to answer her call, Gregory."

"Marissa, don't start."

"You said last night we were done pretending."

"I'm not pretending. I can't control who calls me."

Marissa crossed her arms, the movement small but final.

The brightness between them turned brittle.

Gregory pulled off the blanket with a flourish, swung his long legs off the bed and walked out without another word.

In his study, he opened the desk drawer. The adoption forms waited, crisp and accusing. He took up a pen and began filling them in — *Name. Occupation. Marital status.* Each stroke steadier than he felt.

In the kitchen, Marissa cracked eggs into a bowl. The shells broke cleanly, sharp sounds in the new silence. She whisked until her arm ached, the scent of ghee and resolve rising together.

They stayed apart long enough for the tension to cool.

When Gregory reappeared, he lingered in the doorway, his frame taking up space but his presence careful, like a man unsure he still had the right to enter.

"I should've been honest with you about her," he said matter-of-factly. "She flirts. I ignored it and thought that made me noble. It just made me stupid."

Marissa set the whisk down. "And blind."

He nodded. "Completely. But not unfaithful."

The quiet that followed was different—heavy, but breathable.

She turned the burner down, not looking at him. "You can pour the coffee."

He hesitated for a fraction of a moment, then moved to do as she directed.

The scent of coffee rose between them, a fragile buffer against the morning's emotional chill. Gregory realized the heat had been running for a while—quiet, steady, unnoticed until now.

He sat at the counter, fingers wrapped around a mug he wasn't drinking from. Marissa plated the pancakes, her movements deliberate, careful—like someone rebuilding trust one fluffy disc at a time.

He finally said, "These look good."

"They'll taste better if you stop staring at them like they're your guilt made manifest and pour the syrup."

He pushed the syrup aside in favor of his glucose tablets. The smallest smile bloomed briefly on his face. "I'm sorry about earlier. About the call, about the years before it. I didn't see how much space I left you to fill because of the words I did not say."

She took her seat across from him. "Apologies are easy because it's just us right now. When tomorrow comes and the world pulls us apart again... what then?"

He looked down at his plate, then right at her, locking eyes with hers. "Marissa, I meant what I said last night.

I'm going to be relentless about it — speaking plainly, telling you things, being with you. I have to."

"That sounds exhausting."

"More exhausting than losing you? No, ma'am."

She studied him for a long moment. "You always did make persistence sound romantic."

"It's all I've got left," he said, finishing a pancake in one determined bite. He caught her watching him and froze, remembering what she had said last night about his chewing. Gregory covered his mouth, half-laughing, half-choking. "Persistence," he managed, after swallowing. "And pancakes."

A small laugh escaped her, unexpected and real.

"And for what it's worth — these might be the best pancakes I've ever had."

Getting serious again, Marissa said, "You know, for years I thought love was supposed to feel effortless."

"So did I. But maybe effort is the proof."

They ate quietly for a while, enjoying the easy domestic rhythm they hadn't known in years. Outside, snow slid from the roof in slow sheets; inside, something almost like calm settled between them.

Gregory broke it gently. "What are you thinking?"

"I'm thinking," she said, "that if we ever host another fundraiser, you'd better dance with me. No excuses about tuxedos or small talk."

He blinked. "That's your condition for reconciliation?"

"One of them." She sipped her coffee. "I'm making a list."

He leaned back, exhaling, this time without acrimony or calculation. "Good. Make it long. Gives me something to work for."

Better Than Being Strangers

..⊕ · ❉ ● ▷

"You're drying the dishes wrong," Marissa said.

Gregory looked up from the towel. "There's a wrong way?"

"There's your way."

For a heartbeat, they both waited for the old rhythm—the sigh, the sharp retort, the quiet withdrawal that usually followed. It didn't come. The Sunday stillness felt strange, as if the house itself were holding its breath.

Marissa turned back to the sink, her fingers tracing the edge of the granite. The counter caught the light, flecks of black and white glimmering in the gray surface she'd once resented. It looked different this morning—less like a compromise, more like proof that even imperfect choices could grow on you.

Behind her, Gregory stacked the last plate. "That's it," he said, almost proud.

"Almost," she murmured, reaching for the dish towel to correct his folding.

He grinned, recognizing the tease, and the moment held—briefly ordinary, but entirely new.

His phone rang again.

He froze mid-motion. The screen lit up with the word **MOM.**

Marissa almost smiled. *Of course.*

"Go on," she said, crossing her arms. "You know she won't stop until you answer."

Gregory hesitated, then pressed **accept.**

"Hey, Ma."

Her voice carried, rich with practiced affection for her one and only son. *"Gregory, thank God you're alive. I saw the news. Snow up to the rooftops!"*

"We're fine."

"Oh yes, Marissa? Did she manage?"

"She's right here," he said, glancing toward his wife. "We're both fine."

A pause. "Well, praise be. I told the ladies in prayer group—sometimes the Lord needs to shut off the lights so people can see each other properly again."

Marissa arched an eyebrow. Gregory gave a small, weary laugh.

"So," Delores continued, "any news you'd like to share? Maybe about grandchildren?"

The old Gregory would have changed the subject. The newer one didn't.

"Mom," he said evenly, "that's not your concern. And it's not something you get to use to measure us."

A silence followed, sharp as cracked ice.

"Well," she sniffed, "you don't have to be rude about it."

"I'm not. I want to be clear."

He glanced at Marissa, who was watching him with cautious admiration. "I love you, but we're figuring things out in our own time. You'll know when there's news. Until then, maybe you can pray for our patience instead."

"Patience and prayer I can do," Delores replied, a little mollified. "But I'm adding gratitude if you two actually make it to church next week."

"Fair enough, Ma." Gregory smiled. "We'll try not to make God work overtime."

She laughed softly. *"Love you, baby."*

"Love you too, Ma."

Marissa raised an eyebrow. "That sounded almost civil."

"Growth," he said, drying his hands. "I didn't even check my work messages while she was talking."

"Miracles everywhere."

He leaned a hip against the counter. "You know what I usually do after Sunday breakfast?"

"Spreadsheet review. Color-coded anxiety."

"Exactly. But today, I'm not opening my laptop. Let Monday fend for itself."

She tilted her head, intrigued. "And what will you do instead?"

"Start practicing whatever this is—being present, I guess."

Marissa opened her calendar, thumb hovering over a line of appointments. Then, one by one, she deleted three.

"Work avoidance," she said simply. "If you can take a morning off, so can I."

"A morning?" he teased. "That's all I get?"

"Don't ruin the miracle," she said, smiling.

He disappeared briefly into the study and returned holding the same stack of adoption papers he'd filled out earlier. He placed them on the counter in front of Marissa.

"If I'm going to break a habit," he said, "Our family takes precedence over spreadsheets."

Marissa wrung her hands slowly and looked at the forms, the black ink already smudged in one corner where his thumb had rested. "You finished them."

"Not all the signatures," he said. "Didn't seem right to do it alone."

She met his eyes. "Then don't."

He nodded, slow and certain, and slid the papers toward her.

"No pressure," he said quietly. "They can sit right here until we're both ready."

She reached for a magnet from the fridge — the one shaped like a cardinal — and pinned the papers up. "Then they'll remind us," she said. "Every morning."

The sunlight caught the page, bright and unwavering, as if the day itself had signed witness.

Ding! Ding! Ding!

The loud doorbell freaked them out after someone knocked and rang it like crazy.

Gregory strode to the door and looked through the side window: a neighborhood kid, shovel in hand.

"I'll get it," he said, reaching for his wallet.

Marissa followed Gregory, and they met the boy at the door. "Your timing is perfect," she said.

Gregory asked in an authoritative, no-nonsense tone, "How much for the driveway?"

The kid, unimpressed, shrugged. "Whatever you think it's worth, mister."

Marissa smiled. "That's a dangerous thing to tell a banker and a social worker."

When the door shut again, Gregory was watching her—something tender in his gaze. "You were born to mother, you know that?"

She shook her head. "Don't get poetic before lunch."

"Too late."

They stood by the window, watching the boy work, flinging arcs of snow into the clean white air. He couldn't have been more than twelve, thin under an oversized parka, a red wool hat slipping over one eye. Each shovel heaved more snow onto the pile than off it, the mound already taller than he was.

Gregory smiled. "He's fighting a losing battle."

"He's winning it one scoop at a time," Marissa said.

The boy stumbled, laughed at himself, and kept going. Something in the sight, the effort, the persistence, made them both fall silent again.

"Dinner with your mother," she said suddenly.

He groaned. "We just survived a blizzard."

"Then you can survive her. We'll invite her over next Sunday. Our table, our rules."

"You sure?"

"I'm not afraid of her anymore."

He nodded, quiet admiration in his eyes. "You shouldn't be. We face her as one."

Marissa looked out at the clearing driveway. "She can bring dessert," she added.

He laughed, low and surprised. "You're full of mercy this morning."

"No, I'm full of coffee and pancakes. Mercy's extra."

They fell into a comfortable silence, watching the sun's rays bounce off the snow and shine on the little helper, who was doing his best to make a way for them.

Gregory reached for her hand. She didn't pull away.

Every Day Love

..∞ · ❉ ❥ ▷

"Marissa?"

"Yeah?"

"Stay."

A truck rattled past outside, probably emergency services checking the damage several hours later. Christmas lights still twinkled faintly on porches, their colors dulled by daylight and ice. They remained wrapped in each other after a Sunday-afternoon nap. The real world was reviving itself, intruding on their snow-globe moment. Soon, more neighbors would emerge, shovels scraping, power crews restoring the careful distances electricity allowed.

"Ask me after dinner," she said. "You promised to cook for me. After we remember how to talk to each other — like we did when we were newlyweds. Ask me after the new habits stick. Ask me then."

"You're stalling."

"I'm testing. We're good in a crisis, Gregory. Always have been. It's the every day that breaks us. So let's try *every day* for a while before we make promises we can't keep."

He nodded slowly. "That's fair. But remember, I'm still calling in sick."

"Yes. And I've canceled my morning meetings."

"Look at us. Choosing each other over obligations."

"Don't get cocky. It's day one."

"It's a start."

They untangled themselves from the comforter. Gregory's back cracked audibly as he stood. Marissa's neck had a crick that would need heat to resolve. They were too old for dramatic reconciliations, too set in their ways for easy transformation. But maybe that was the point. Maybe this was what genuine love looked like at forty-something — less fireworks, more endurance.

"I'll start the laundry," Marissa offered.

"I'll start dinner."

"Gregory?"

He paused in the doorway. "Yeah?"

"The divorce papers. They're in my laptop bag. Whatever happens today or tomorrow, I need you to know they exist. That I was that close. That this isn't just storm drama or temporary insanity. I was leaving."

"I know."

"You know?"

"Your sister called me last week. Said you'd been looking at apartments. Asked if I was really going to let you go without a fight."

"You didn't say or do anything."

He nodded once. "I didn't know how to fight for something I'd already lost."

She swallowed. "And now?"

"Now I know we hadn't lost it — just buried it under silence and habit and fear of being honest. I kept thinking if I worked harder, kept doing what I was doing, it would somehow fix itself." He met her eyes. "I was wrong. So now, I'm going to pour all those conversations I've been practicing in my head right into the real world. All over you. Are you ready?"

Marissa tried not to smile. "You make it sound simple."

"No," he said. "I mean to make it sound necessary. There's a difference."

The room brightened as late-day light pooled across the floor, catching the framed photos on the console — trips, birthdays, proof that they'd once been effortless. For the first time in years, she didn't feel mocked by them. A strand of half-lit garland sagged along the console, one bulb stubbornly flashing red. A forgotten mug of cocoa sat cold beside it. She would need to fix that garland before Christmas Eve.

"I need to say something," Marissa began. "About last night, today —"

"Don't." Gregory half turned. "Whatever you're about to say to create distance, to protect yourself, to hedge bets... don't."

"I was going to say thank you."

He blinked, surprised. "Oh."

"Thank you for fighting when I'd already started packing in my head. For making space where there wasn't any. For not letting the quiet win."

Gregory crossed back to her, slow and sure. "Then thank God for that snow storm. Thank you for lingering long enough for me to figure it out."

She stood and reached for him, fingertips brushing the front of his shirt. "You still owe me dinner."

He smiled. "I was thinking pasta. The kind that sticks to the pan because I never stir it enough."

"I'll bring the wine."

After she had loaded the washing machine, she picked a Cabernet from the wine cellar and joined him in the kitchen.

They moved around each other — first awkward, then finding rhythm. He opened the pantry, scanning shelves that hadn't been properly stocked since Thanksgiving, and picked. A jar of sun-dried tomatoes. Linguine. Half a bottle of olive oil. Garlic bulbs going soft at the edges.

"Looks like we still have that jar of nutmeg from the Christmas cookies you swore you'd bake," he teased, holding it up.

Gregory rolled his sleeves, tossed the garlic into the air theatrically, caught it, slapped it on the counter, then crushed it with the flat of a knife. Marissa rolled her eyes and did not struggle too hard to hide her amusement.

"Show off."

The scent filled the kitchen almost instantly. He'd forgotten how much he loved this part — the hiss of oil meeting heat, the comfort of creation. He hadn't really cooked in months, not since their fights turned every meal into a hostile negotiation.

Marissa leaned against the counter, watching him. "You remember what you're doing?"

He grinned over his shoulder. "It's like riding a bike. A very garlicky bike."

When he drained the pasta, steam rose and clouded the window. He tossed it all together — pasta, tomatoes, Parmesan, the last of their basil plant that had barely survived the winter. He plated two portions, wiped the rims like he used to when he tried to impress her, and carried them to the table.

The smell was home itself.

Marissa twirled a forkful, blew gently, and took a bite. For a second, she just closed her eyes. "You're an excellent cook," she purred.

"I used to be."

"You still are." She took another bite, slower this time. "Maybe you should do this more often."

He looked up, amused. "Cook dinner or make you lick your lips?"

"Both. But start with cooking."

For a while, they ate in silence — good silence, not the kind that used to press between them. Then Gregory set down his fork.

"Do you still love me?" he asked quietly. "Not the memory of me, not the potential of me. This me. Right here, right now, with all my failures and fears and stupid 5 A.M. gym sessions."

Marissa looked at him in the soft light of the candles they'd found under the sink. She saw the gray in his beard, the lines that mapped two decades of stress, the eyes that still held traces of the boy who'd carried her books when she was doing her master's in sociology. Saw the stranger he'd become and the friend he'd been, the provider who'd lost his way and maybe the partner trying to find it back.

"Yes," she said simply. "God help me, yes. Not the same as twenty years ago. That was easier love, cleaner. This is complicated. Has conditions and pointed edges and an entire catalog of disappointments. But it's also deeper. Knows the cost of staying. Chooses anyway."

He exhaled. "Even with how I chew?"

"Jury's still out on that."

He laughed, and she joined him, their shoulders shaking, pasta forgotten. When the laughter ebbed, he reached across the table, brushing her hand with his thumb.

"You know," he said, "we never made a contingency plan."

"For?"

"If the pipes froze. If the roof leaks. If the basement floods. We're completely unprepared."

"Story of our marriage."

He shook his head. "No. Story of our marriage is we prepared for the wrong things. Financial security, social standing, professional success. Just forgot to prepare for how to stay in love when life got complicated."

"So what's our contingency plan for that?"

Gregory thought for a moment. "Wednesday night dinners. Non-negotiable. Phones off, real food, conversation that goes deeper than logistics. If we can't make Wednesday, we make it up within forty-eight hours."

"Sunday morning walks. Before your gym time. Just us, no podcasts or calls. Walking and talking like we used to."

"Monthly state of the union," he added. "We sit down, say what's working, what's not, what needs attention. No letting things fester until they explode."

"You're making us sound like a business merger."

"Better than a dissolution. Besides, good marriages need structure too. Not to contain them but to support them. Like those trellises you wanted for the garden we never planted."

"We should plant that garden."

"Add it to the list. Garden, kids, pottery, actual conversation. We'll be busy."

"Better than being strangers."

Gregory reached for her hand again, palm to palm. "Better than being strangers," he reflected.

The candles burned low beside the small decorative wreath. Outside, the snow softened to rain. Inside, they stacked plates in the sink and talked about next week's

groceries, the way people do when they've decided to
stay.

Epilogue — Six Months Later

..∞ · ✷ ☙ ▷

The Shape of Love

The pottery wheel spun, clay sliding through Marissa's fingers as she tried to center it. Beside her, Gregory was having worse luck, his third attempt at a bowl looking more like abstract art.

"You're thinking too hard," she said.

"I'm an overthinker. You knew this when you married me."

"When I married you, you overthought different things."

"True. Hey, did you call the adoption agency back?"

"This morning. Our home visit is scheduled for next month."

"Next month?" His voice cracked slightly. "That's soon."

"That's decades in the making, but who's counting?" She glanced at him, saw the familiar panic starting. "Breathe. We've got time to prepare."

"I've been preparing since our night in the dark. Doesn't feel like enough."

"It never will. That's what everyone says. You just jump and build wings on the way down."

"Mixed metaphor."

"Shut up and make your bowl."

They worked in companionable silence, the studio filled with other couples trying to create something from nothing. Their instructor, a serene woman named Beth who'd seen them through many failed attempts, stopped by their stations.

"You get distracted mid-throw, don't you?"

"Story of my brain," Marissa muttered.

"You're doing better. You're learning to let the clay be what it wants. I see you. Tuning in."

"And you," Beth turned to Gregory, "need to stop trying to control every molecule. Clay doesn't respond to pressure like that."

"I don't apply pressure for everything," he protested.

Marissa leaned closer, murmuring to Beth, "He brought a notepad. With goals for 'healthy emotional elasticity'."

"Traitor."

"He color-coded the feelings."

"It was helpful!"

"It was insane," she said, laughing. "But also sweet. Insanely sweet."

Beth moved on, hiding a smile. They'd become her favorite disaster, these two who showed up every week ready to fail better than last time. Gregory abandoned his lopsided bowl and started fresh. Marissa's cylinder was actually holding shape.

"Remember our first class?" she asked.

"You mean when I wore my gym clothes and got clay all over them?"

"You were so proud of those moisture-wicking fabrics."

"They wicked moisture. Just not clay."

"You know what I love?"

"That I've stopped wearing gym clothes to pottery?"

"That you came. That you show up every week even though you're terrible at it."

"We're both terrible at it."

"Yeah, but I enjoy being terrible. You're constitutionally opposed to being bad at things."

"I'm learning. Turns out being bad at pottery with you is better than being good at investment portfolios alone."

"Speaking of portfolios - did you talk to Davidson about reducing your client load?"

"Meeting's tomorrow. He won't be happy."

"You don't need his permission to have a life, Gregory."

"I know. Old habits."

"How's the new habit coming?"

He smiled, that softer expression she'd been seeing more often. "Good. Weird, but good. Who knew lunch breaks were for actual lunch?"

"Revolutionary concept."

"My trainer thinks I'm having an affair."

"Why?"

"Because I've been skipping morning sessions to have breakfast with my wife. Apparently that's more suspicious than actual affairs."

"We live in a broken world."

"We're fixing our corner of it."

The truth of that settled between them, solid as the clay they worked. Not fixed — never that. It would take years, maybe forever. But *fixing* — present tense, active verb. Breakfast conversations that wandered. Walks through the neighborhood, the kind that drew quiet stares from neighbors seeing them together perhaps for the first time in a decade. Therapy sessions that left them raw but somehow closer.

"I love you," Gregory said suddenly.

"In public? Who are you?"

"I'm your man, in this class and in life."

"I love you too."

Her cylinder collapsed, clay folding in on itself. Marissa laughed instead of cursing, starting over. That was progress, too — finding humor in failure, knowing it wasn't the end.

"Hey," Gregory said quietly. "What would you think about renewing our vows? Nothing big. Just us, family, acknowledging who we are now instead of who we thought we'd be."

"You want a do-over?"

"No. I want a do-better. Want to promise things that actually matter. Like coming home. Like choosing each other when it's hard. Like understanding that love at twenty-three looks different than love at forty-three, but it's love."

"Can we write our own vows this time?"

"Wouldn't have it any other way."

"Then yes. But after the adoption goes through. I want our kids there."

"Our kids," he repeated, wonder in his voice. "I can't believe we're finally doing it."

"Believe it. And believe they're going to destroy our perfect house."

"Good. It was never meant to be perfect. Only ours."

The wheel spun, clay formed and reformed, and two people who'd almost lost everything continued the patient work of building something new from the remnants of what was. Not perfect, not easy, but theirs. Always theirs.

..∞ · ♥ · →→

THE END

If *Love In The Dark* held your heart, *Scarlet Yearnings: Beyond First Glance* will keep it company. Discover twelve stories of second looks, second chances, and love seen clearly.

•••

Get Scarlet Yearnings

A Note from the Author

Thank you for reading!

Your support means the world to me.

If you enjoyed Love in the Dark: A Holiday Romance
For Grown-Ups:

PLEASE LEAVE A REVIEW ON GOODREADS AND AMAZON.

•••

Review Love in the Dark

Your feedback helps other readers find their next
favorite read and inspires me to keep writing stories
that resonate with you. – Scarlet Ibis James

About the Author

Scarlet Ibis James is an award-winning contemporary romance author who infuses her stories with the warmth of her Trinidadian heritage and the electric energy of New York City, where she now resides. Having weathered a decade of Connecticut winters—complete with blizzards and power outages—she knows firsthand how isolation can illuminate truth.

James crafts delightfully flawed, deeply human characters who mirror her own blend of zest and introspection. Her engaging narratives explore the complexities of love, self-discovery, and life's unexpected turns, all delivered with humor, heart, and touches of magical realism.

A believer in hard-won happy endings, James writes for readers who like their romance with emotional honesty and their love stories earned rather than given.

Author Website: scarletibisjames.com

◎ g ⓕ

Also by Scarlet Ibis James

Love. Legacy. Second chances.

Scarlet Ibis James writes contemporary stories about people rediscovering connection after distance — where tenderness is work, desire is honest, and hope is hard-won.

If you enjoyed *Love in the Dark: A Holiday Romance for Grown-Ups,* you'll find more heartfelt journeys in these books →

Scarlet Yearnings: Stories of Love and Desire

Twelve stories. Twelve women. One shared longing.

In *Scarlet Yearnings,* award-winning author Scarlet Ibis James captures Black women at the tender edge of desire, when love is hoped for, withheld, mishandled, or just out of reach.

These intimate stories follow women navigating vanished lovers, quiet betrayals, emotional mismatches, and the ache of wanting more than they are offered. Each character feels familiar, not because she is predictable, but because her hunger for connection rings true.

Unflinching and deeply compassionate, this collection honors women who keep choosing love, even when experience tells them to be careful. These are stories for readers who believe longing is not weakness, and that wanting deeply is its own kind of courage.

For readers who savor emotional truth, complex women, and love that refuses to be simple.

https://scarletibisjames.com/books

Scarlet Yearnings: Beyond First Glance

Trade Book Cover

After the spark, what remains?

In *Scarlet Yearnings: Beyond First Glance*, Scarlet Ibis James turns her lens to love after attraction, after mistakes, after the easy answers have fallen away.

Told through the perspectives of both women and men, these twelve stories explore what happens when relationships are tested by time, regret, illness, distance, and the quiet labor of staying. Set across Trinidad, Toronto, Washington, D.C., and imagined futures, the collection asks harder questions about forgiveness, commitment, and emotional honesty.

Tender yet unsentimental, these stories reveal love not as fantasy, but as a daily choice. One that demands bravery, humility, and the willingness to begin again.

For readers who know the real story of love starts after the first glance.

https://scarletibisjames.com/books

Scarlet Birthright: What They Left Behind

Some absences shape a lifetime.

In *Scarlet Birthright*, Joromi Enoch leaves Trinidad for America chasing respectability and approval, and in doing so abandons his young daughter, Trisha. As Joromi builds a life that excludes his firstborn, Trisha grows up carrying the weight of his absence, shaping her sense of worth, love, and belonging.

Years later, father and daughter are forced to reckon with what was lost, what was chosen, and what may still be possible. This emotionally resonant story examines how parental choices echo across generations, and whether redemption can exist without erasing harm.

An award-winning and shortlisted novella, *Scarlet Birthright* has been recognized for its unflinching exploration of family, diaspora, and generational healing.

Intimate, searching, and quietly devastating, *Scarlet Birthright* is a story about inheritance, accountability, and the complicated love that survives even when family fractures.

For readers drawn to literary fiction about family, diaspora, and the long work of healing.

https://scarletibisjames.com/books